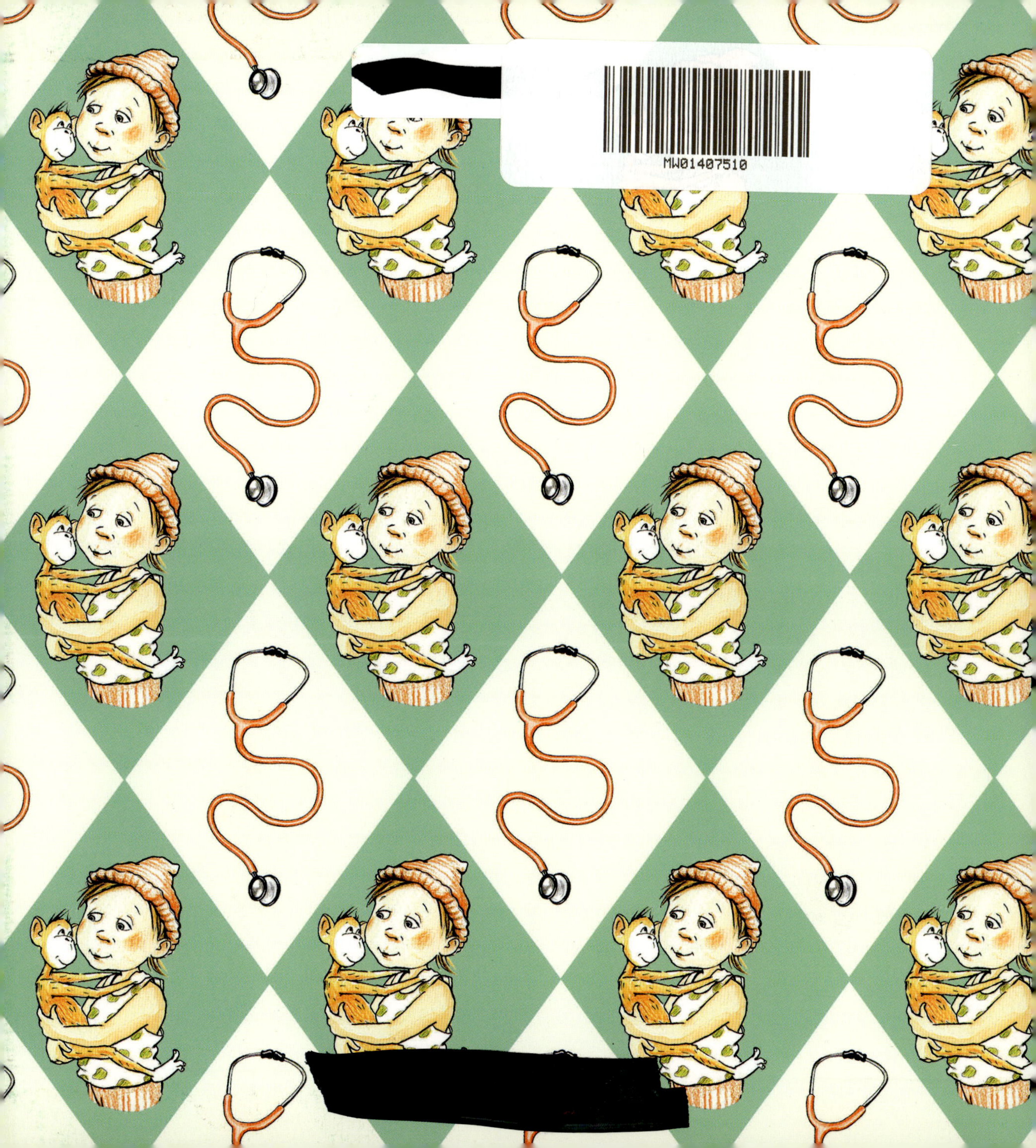

Ellis Goes to the Doctor

Written by Siri Reuterstrand
Illustrated by Jenny Wik

Sky Pony Press • New York

Copyright © 2012 by Siri Reuterstrand and Jenny Wik

Originally published as ELLIS GÅR TIL DOKTORN
© *Siri Reuterstrand (text) and Jenny Wik (illustrations), 2007*
Published by agreement with B Wahlströms Bokförlag, Forma Books AB, Sweden
Translated by Monika Romare

All Rights Reserved. No part of this book may be reproduced in any manner without the express written consent of the publisher, except in the case of brief excerpts in critical reviews or articles. All inquiries should be addressed to Sky Pony Press, 307 West 36th Street, 11th Floor, New York, NY 10018.

Sky Pony Press books may be purchased in bulk at special discounts for sales promotion, corporate gifts, fund-raising, or educational purposes. Special editions can also be created to specifications. For details, contact the Special Sales Department, Sky Pony Press, 307 West 36th Street, 11th Floor, New York, NY 10018 or info@skyhorsepublishing.com.

Sky Pony® is a registered trademark of Skyhorse Publishing, Inc.®, a Delaware corporation.

Visit our website at www.skyponypress.com.

10 9 8 7 6 5 4 3 2 1

Manufactured in China, March 2012
This product conforms to CPSIA 2008

Library of Congress Cataloging-in-Publication Data is available on file.

ISBN: 978-1-61608-662-6

Normally, Ellis likes to run around and play all day long. But not today.

It all began with a fever and a runny nose.

Then Ellis slept most of the day.

A few days later Ellis felt a little bit better and he stayed up playing again.

But then the cough came. Most of the time it came in the evenings and at night, when Ellis was supposed to be sleeping.

Nobody at home got much sleep at all.
Not Ellis, not Mom, not even Dad.

One morning, Dad had had enough.
"It is time to go to the doctor," Dad said.

At the doctor's office, Ellis and his dad had to wait for a while.

Ellis thought it was strange that there were so many toys there.

All the kids that come to see the doctor are sick. *How are you supposed to be playing when you are sick?* thought Ellis. At least Ballowits was having fun on the little slide.

Finally, a woman came and asked Ellis and his dad to follow her into a room.

"I am going to examine you," she said, "so that I can find out what is making you sick."

"I am going to start by examining your nose. I will poke inside of it with a stick. It might feel a bit funny, but it won't hurt."

Ellis had to sit on his hands while the nurse poked around in his nose. Blah! It itched in a strange way.

Ellis got a little teary-eyed, but it didn't hurt. The nurse was telling the truth about that.

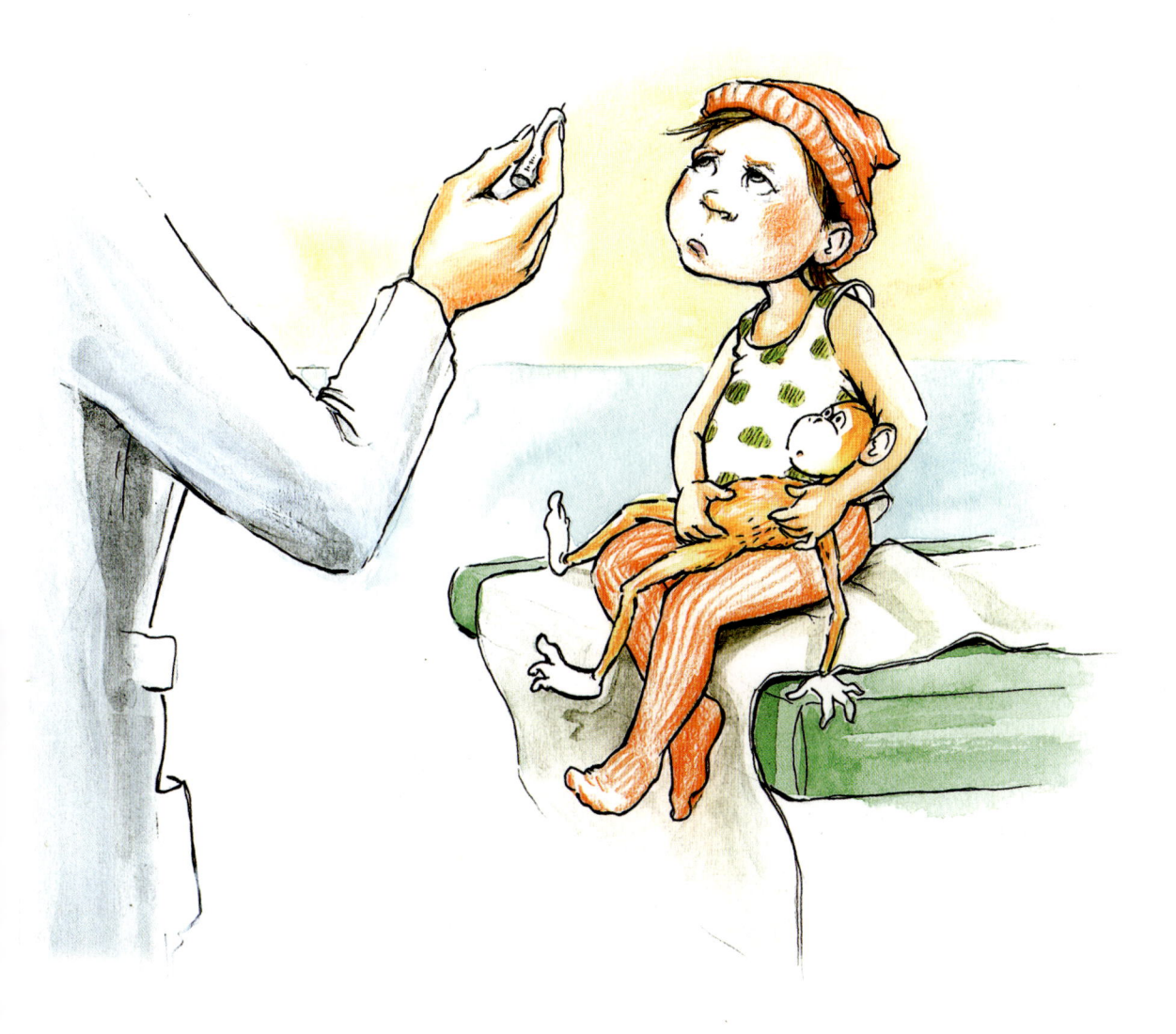

"And I want to prick you in the finger too. It will be really quick," the nurse told him.

Ellis started to feel a bit annoyed with her.

"You can prick Ballowits," he told her.
"I can do that first and then prick you. I will give you a nice band-aid afterwards," the nurse told him.

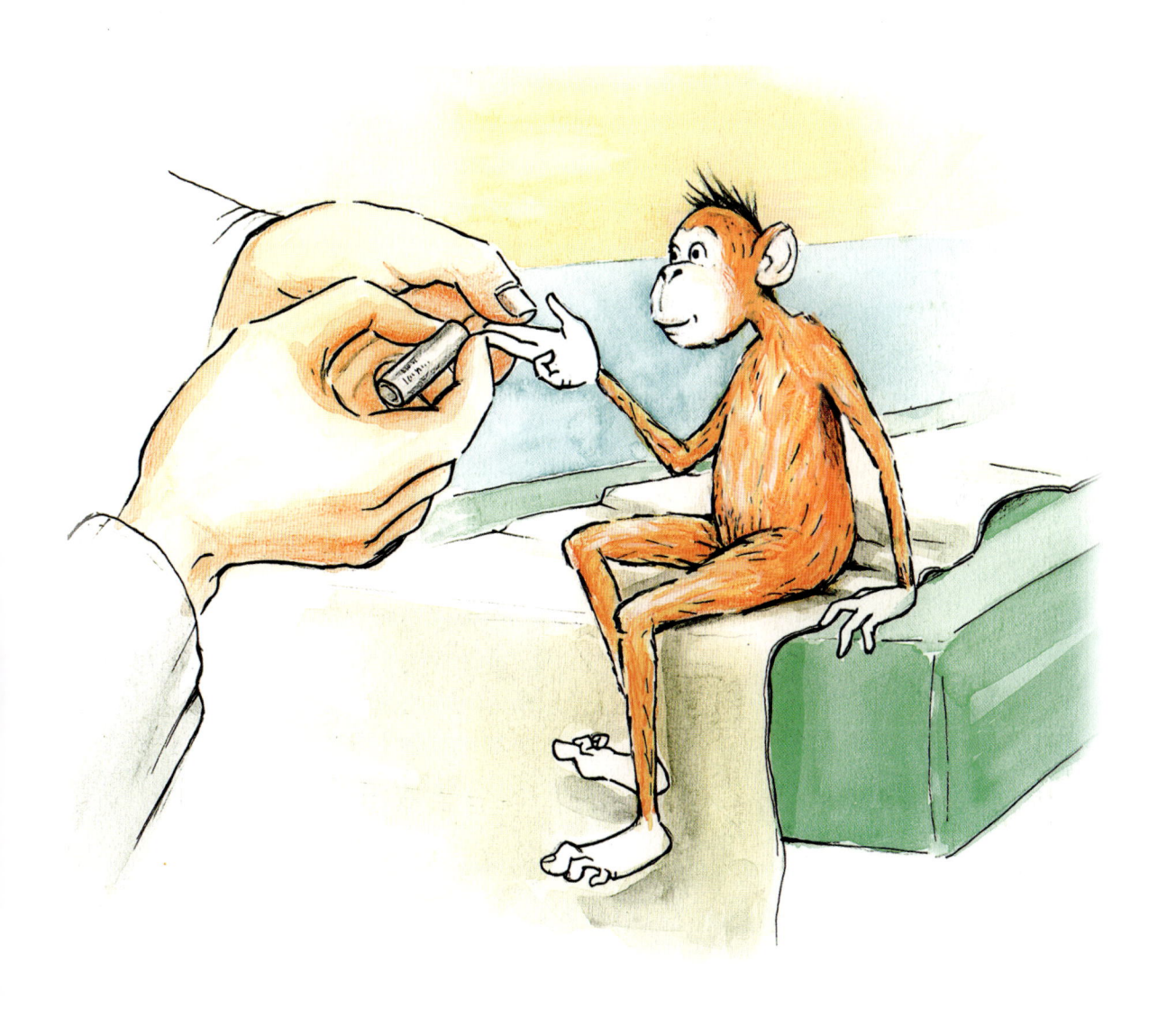

"Okay!" said Ellis.
If Ballowits is brave enough, I am brave enough, Ellis thought.

When the nurse was done examining Ellis, the doctor came in.
While she was speaking with Dad, Ellis put a band-aid on Ballowits too.
The nurse had forgotten about that.

The doctor then wanted to listen to Ellis's chest.
"Take a deep inhale, please," she said.
"What?" Ellis asked.
"Like this," the doctor said and breathed in air through her mouth.
Then Ellis understood and kept breathing and breathing.

Then it was time to listen to his back.

"Can you cough a little bit?" the doctor asked.

Ellis had become really good at coughing the past few days, so that was not an issue.

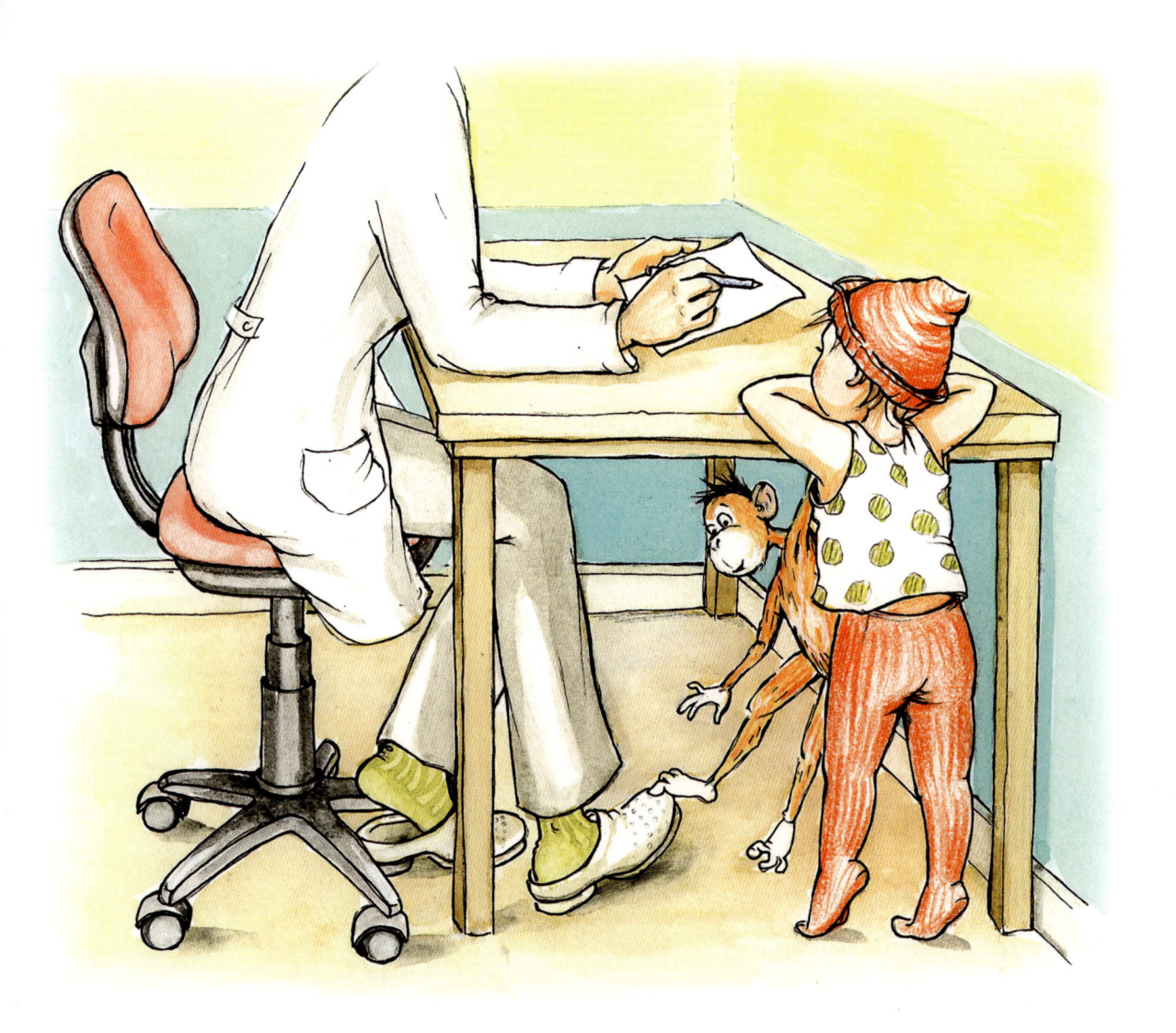

"I will write you a prescription for some cough medicine, so that you can sleep," the doctor said.

"You will feel better soon. But you must stay away from babies for a while, and you probably shouldn't go to daycare."

Dad bought the cough medicine on the way home. The bottle was big and brown. It came with a little cup that Dad needed to measure the medicine in. It was supposed to be measured to the first line. Three times a day.

It didn't taste very good, but Ellis was good and swallowed it anyway.

That night everyone slept really well.
It won't be very long before Ellis feels well again.

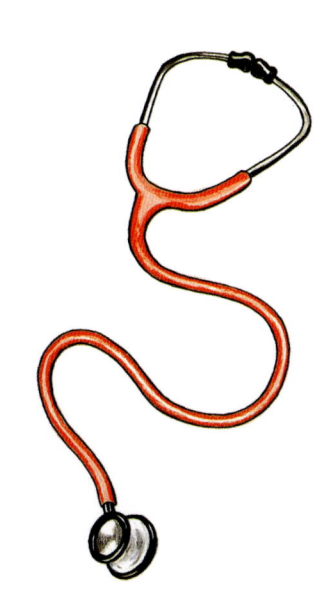

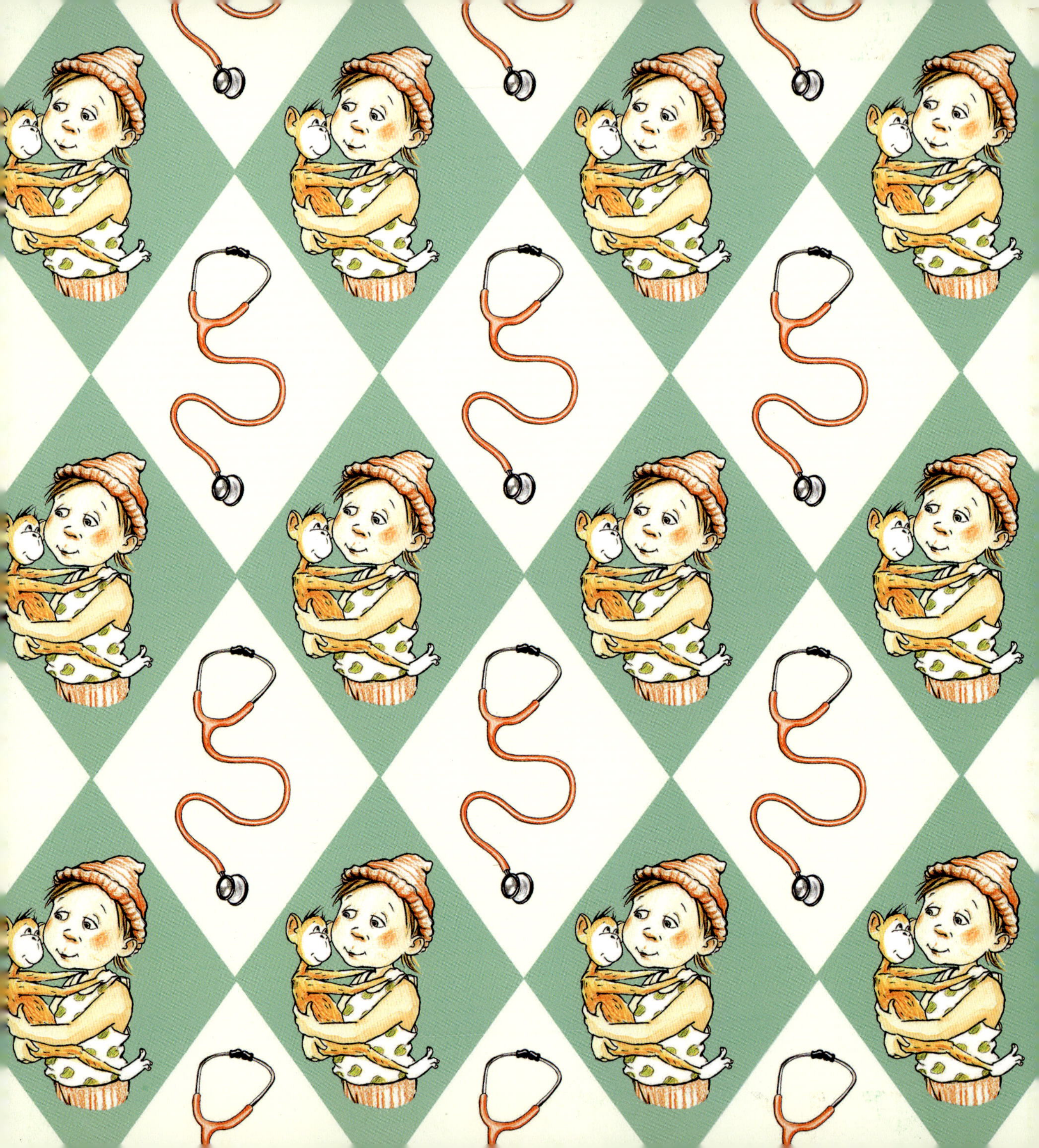